FOREVER AGO

SUSHAMA KARNIK

Contents

Foreword

I want these stories to evolve in the reader's mind as he/ she will walk away taking with them the memories of the moments they will have shared with these characters. Let them, in their happiness and sadness, recall those shared experiences like the feel of sand slipping out of their fingers, slightly hurting, strangely soft. At such moments, let the ill-tempered man or woman who might be troubling them inside, calm down in the sudden realisation of love. Life is an open beach to explore waves, the rains, the sunshine, storms, and peace.

Emma, Forever Ago

It was humid throughout the day. Soon I had to move on from here and go back home, but still a month to go. Considering the three long years I was posted here for the training as marine engineer, one month now seemed like a day. With nothing much to do now; this sudden respite felt like a push-over from the buzz of insanity into a suffocating silence.

Vancouver is generally peaceful. It is a town nestled among hills and the sea and is covered by persistent drizzle. That accounts for the feeling of gloom that settles over outsiders like me who cannot find the pulse of the life in this town. That was a particularly cranky day when the sky and the weather were stubbornly gloomy and grey. After breakfast I had to find something to occupy myself till lunch and that was a pretty long interval. There were two antique bookshops on the street behind my lodging. I always felt at home in the one which had at its counter a rather perennially tired shop-assistant who watched over the entire shop from her dark gothic looking corner, with an equally gothic looking cat to give her company.

Whenever I tried to open a conversation with the lady the cat would snarl viciously from behind the counter to block any further potential or real overtures from the unwelcome alien that was me. Needless to say that I always ignored both and went straight to the bookshelves.

That day a notice stuck on the window pane caught my eye and I stopped to read it. It was an announcement of a book-exhibition that was housed in a small public-hall around the next corner. I threw a glance at the inside of the book-shop. The unappealing sight of the gothic cat and its dumb owner hastened to help me make up my mind in favour of the book-exhibition around the corner which was not too far from where I was standing.

By the time I started walking in the new direction, the drizzle was piercingly sharp, with the wind sweeping past my coat and umbrella with an impatient bustle. As I entered the hall, to my surprise, I found that the exhibition was to start on the next day; I had overlooked this bit of information in my eagerness to find out a new haunt.

In the meantime, the place was occupied by a group of young choir children practising singing for the Sunday at Church. By that time, it was raining so heavily outside that there was no point in venturing out again in the rains. So I hung my coat and the umbrella on the stand in the corner and selected one of the chairs in the front row.

On the rostrum, seated in three compact rows of auditorium chairs, were about twenty children, mostly girls, ranging in age from about seven to thirteen. At the first signal given to them by their instructor who looked all pervasive because of her imposing manners and strident voice, the children looked at one another in bewilderment. Some of them opened their mouth, but were still afraid to articulate the sound, not sure if the others were ready to share the effort. Some of them tried to be clever and just put on an ingratiating smile. With exhortation from the coach to start and be audible they mouthed the words without the necessary feeling. The coach now thought it best not to waste time on further exhortation, blew a note on her pipe and the children raised their hymn-books above their heads for a second, and then resuming their normal posture, started singing in unison. They sang with the unsentimental innocence natural to their age. I had never heard the hymn before, but it had a soothing quality and a healing effect; I wished it not to end soon.

Listening, I drifted in thought and scanned those young faces absent-mindedly. The child nearest me was in the front row of the group. Well, not exactly a child; she looked about somewhere between fourteen and sixteen, with straight black hair cut to shoulder length, which stuck around her forehead because wet, making her face look unglamorous and common. But as I continued to listen, I noticed that her voice was distinctly superior to others. It was sweet-sounding, and because it was the surest, it naturally led the others.

However, the young lady seemed to be indifferent to the activity she was engaged in at the time because I saw her controlling an overpowering yawn once. It was a closed- mouth, lady-like yawn, but her nostrils gave it away. Her eyes had no expression at all except perhaps that of being unimpressed because of over-familiarity. Once or twice she seemed to scan the people in the audience with a casual interest that did not amount to curiosity, except as if she was counting the heads. For a fraction of a moment she took notice of me and I felt out of place occupying the seat in the front row. Perhaps she understood my embarrassment and graciously looked away. The moment the singing stopped the choir children became impatient to get away from the scrutiny and criticism of the coach and the audience, though to my tired nerves their performance was more than what I could rate. Their coach was in no mind to let them slip out so soon. She began to give her lengthy opinion on how some children can't remain still and composed while rehearsing. That was the time I realized that my presence in the front row was going to invite the hostility of the children and the censure of their teacher. The hymn was definitely over and I did not want the coach's dissonant voice to break the spell the children's singing had cast upon me. I got up hastily and left the hall.

Outside on the street the things were far more difficult than when I had stepped inside the hall. It was raining harder. I put on my raincoat and crossed the street and found refuge in a coffee-shop. It was my first visit to that shop and while I was looking for the coat-stand around, the matronly looking owner of the shop gave me a look as if she would have preferred a customer with a drier appearance. Not to give her offence, I took as much care as I could to see that my dripping raincoat made as little mess as possible.

As I sat down at my table with my tray of coffee and toast I saw the young lady at the choir entering in and taking off her coat. I noticed that she was not alone. She was accompanied by an elderly looking lady and a little impish-looking guy who was probably her younger brother. They occupied a table not far away from me and fortunately I was able to get an unobstructed view of the entire party. The boy was about five to six years of age, and was in no mood to obey anyone. He started looking around with curiosity to discover some vulnerable target at which he could direct his mischief. Before giving him an opportunity to decide that I could be his potential target, I hastily put on my patent "keep away at safe distance or I know how to tackle brats like you" kind of look. Luckily, they had not yet noticed me watching them.

As they settled down at their table, the boy set about annoying his companions very methodically, giving me an instant insight into the kind of tricks he had mastered rather well. He started rocking in his chair in the most irritating manner, acting as if he was going to pull down the table with the table-cloth and all. The elderly lady advised him once or twice to sit straight but it was only when his sister admonished him in a stern voice that he stuck the small of his back to the chair, but in the meanwhile he dropped the napkin on the floor, picked it up neatly and spread it over his head and sat balancing it dexterously. She did not go to the counter to get their tea. It was brought to them by the waitress.

While they were in the process of pouring tea into their cups, she noticed me suddenly and gave me the same indifferent look with which she had regarded me at the choir-practice.

For the next few moments I remained engrossed in my thoughts which did not have any specific object to feed upon. I was thinking of the letter my wife had written to me some time back and which had reached me on the previous day. It was a long list of grievances about my mother. She wanted me to write to my mother on her behalf. I brushed aside all those concerns for a while, and started enjoying the pitter-patter of the raindrops on the window-sill. I had to finish my coffee and get ready to go. I could not prolong my stay indefinitely long. Before making up my mind to get up, I looked at her and found her looking at me with a certain curiosity. I returned her glance with a seemingly nonchalant look, balancing the act between trying not to offend and trying not to look rudely indifferent either. In that brief moment of awareness, she gave me a faintly visible, qualified little smile. It was oddly radiant as certain unexpected, half-revealed smiles are. I smiled back, less radiantly, taking care that my smile did not carry any unwelcome signs that may cause a misunderstanding. But I was overwhelmed, to be sure.

The next thing I knew was that she was out of her seat and having covered the distance in a few steps she was now standing by my table.

I got up from my seat and requested her to be seated and be comfortable. She bowed slightly and sat down facing me. "Are you from Asia?" She asked after she had made sure with a slight observation that I was a good guy. "I am from India." I replied.

"Oh, then you are a teetotaler I suppose," she said. I watched her for a moment to detect any trace of sarcasm. There was nothing but the freshness of adolescence in her bearing. So I ruled out sarcasm.

She saw through my doubt and while I was fumbling for an answer, she said, "There is nothing wrong in being a teetotaler. Your culture forbids you to drink perhaps." I was not sure whether to tell her that I was not exactly averse to drinking, but I thought it best to let her continue with the impression she had formed; I am more at ease with myself and others when an acquaintance begins with an impression and not with an opinion.

I asked her if she would care to join me. "Yes; for a little while," she said. I got up and drew a chair for her, the one opposite me. I hurried back to my chair. I wanted to hold the thread of conversation but was not sure how to. I finally decided to let her take the lead and sat there facing her quietly, as if for a judgment.

"You were there at the choir-practice; I saw you," she said plainly, without any coquetry. I was impressed by the poise which to my mind was rather remarkable for her age. I admitted I was there and that I was quite impressed by her singing. She nodded and said, "I know." She was not excited over the compliment. There seemed to be a slight shadow of wistfulness in her eyes. She kept looking out at the rain outside and then in a slight whisper, as if talking to herself said, "Choir-singing is not my end really; it's just a stop-over. I want to be a professional singer." Though she showed no eagerness for a response from me, I ventured to say just in order to prolong the opportunity of being with her, though I regretted the moment I said it, "Oh, I would have thought that you were made out to be a nun."

She flashed a glance at me which I felt to be a look of disapproval, if not exactly of anger. "Oh, really? And what made you think so?" she asked with a determination to retaliate what she perceived to be an insinuation at her plain looks. Though that certainly was not what I had in mind, it gave me a secret pleasure to see her annoyed. But it was too fragile a moment to be wasted in silly overtures. I hastened to clarify, "I mean, you sang with such devoutness; it was heavenly." Again a half-smile lit up her face and as if with a glint of comprehension in her eyes she said, "Really? Don't expect me to believe that. I wasn't quite born yesterday, you know?"

I silenced the voice in me that urged me to say, "That was really the truth!"

I had remained a foreigner all these days while I was here in Canada, clinging to my roots back there in India. I knew nothing about Western music and if the talk were to veer around to dwell on Western music I had precious little to say. However, she was warming up to the subject and I thought it convenient to let her unwind.

She said, "I am practising in the choir because that is all I can afford in my circumstances right now. Besides, vocal music does not make demands on your purse. My real passion is piano and guitar, but can't afford."

I looked at her carefully. She had placed her hands in front of her on the table and she was sitting in an upright position as if with her fingers on the keyboard of piano. She had long tapering fingers but the nails were bitten to the quick. Though there was no fidgetiness in her till then she became instantly self-conscious when she found me looking at her fingers. She immediately withdrew her hands and hid them in the pockets of her long skirt.

I offered her a piece of the cinnamon toast which she refused without an excuse. She seemed eager to talk but I could see her companions getting restless and impatient. The lady who accompanied her was making frantic signals for her to end the interaction with a stranger, but she was determined to talk. She moved her chair so as to block her companion out of view and asked me, "Are you interested in Western music?" I said, "I don't understand the trends in music, neither in the West nor in India. I listen if it soothes my nerves"

"How did you find our singing? Was it soothing?" She asked. I was at once struck by the fact that she said 'our singing', not 'my singing'. I realized that she was steeped in the spirit of the choir and had learnt to subdue her personality in the unified voice of the chorus. Perhaps that was the reason why she wanted to carve a niche for herself in piano or guitar. She answered the question in my mind rather surprisingly for me. She said, "Basically I am not cut out for team-work. I am at my best when I work alone." There was very little time at her disposal and she did not know how best to use it. For a girl of her age she seemed rather grownup and sedate. But there was still some glint of silliness in her which showed when she asked impulsively, "Are you married?" I was tempted to say 'no' and watch her reaction. But by now I had begun to like her and refrained from playing games. I liked the spontaneous camaraderie she had begun to feel with me without any reason. I did not want to wreck it by giving a false answer to a question asked trustfully, whatever be its motive. "Yes," I said, "I am married." The next thing I expected her to ask was: "How long?" But she again asked a question that was sillier still. She said, "Are you in love with your wife?"

I gave her a searching look. Perhaps she was brought up to believe that in India, being in love with your spouse is not the demand of married life and that marriages survive without love. However, I thought it best to maintain silence. She did not seem to take my silence very seriously because the question she had asked did not carry weight; it was asked out of a casual interest, to set the ball rolling. But she immediately hastened to say, "Oh, sorry, I am afraid, I am being too personal." I told her that I would bring it to her notice if she was so. She said, "Actually I am not very gregarious, you know?" She stopped and looked at me with a look which I thought rather presumptuous. I was amused to see that she was waiting to see if the word 'gregarious' was there in my vocabulary.

"One of my teachers is into 'Zen,' you know. I am learning the lesson of compassion from 'Zen'. She says that one must feel the vibrations and respond positively. I think those who don't speak that lingo call it being pro-active." I started wondering what compassion and being positive or pro-active had to do with my being married or not. But I did not have to ask. She was quickly forthcoming with the explanation. She said, "You have a very sensitive face. I noticed that you looked lonely." This, if it were to come from any other woman who was a stranger, could have been construed as an innuendo. But I was gradually getting drawn into her world which had a strange fragrance about it.

Without betraying any kind of a reaction to her perception of my state of mind, I told her that I wasn't lonely. However, I said I was glad for her compassion. Just then her brother was heard crying out her name loudly. "Emma, Emma, we are leaving if you don't come soon." I turned to look in his direction and found everyone else looking at us.

She had to get up. She gave me a broad, effusive smile without any sign of embarrassment or apology and said, "Good, Charles introduced me to you. I am Emma and he is Charles, my younger brother.

At that very moment, Charles left his place at the other end of the room and leaving the elderly lady in a state of abandonment, came and joined his sister at our end. I braced myself up for an unexpected calamity as I saw him ready to pull the table-cloth over his head. "Do sit up straight in your chair, Charles." She commanded as she sat down again. "Say hello to uncle..." and she looked at me with a question in her eyes. " Pratap," I said. "Pratap Sharma". Charles of course was not expected to be impressed. He stuck out his tongue and looked up at the ceiling. Emma was a bit apologetic now and said, "Sorry, that's his way of expressing boredom. Don't take it seriously".

However, the little guy had started taking an interest in me. He was in no hurry to make a move now. He put on an angelic face and gave me a nice little hand-shake. It was a welcome sign of warmth but there was no time for us to get to know each other better. Emma signalled in the direction of her aunt to indicate that she was coming and pulled Charles towards her in a hurry.

Charles wanted to make the best use of this fleeting moment of intimacy between him and me and before going away; he turned and asked me, "What did one wall say to another?" I looked at him in a surprise when he said to aid me in answering his question..."It's a riddle." I rolled up my eyes and said with a stumped expression, "I give up!" He pulled his sister in the direction of the table where his aunt was waiting for them and started running. Turning back towards me, he yelled out the answer, "Meet you at the corner!'

After Emma and her companions had left the coffee-shop I sat for a while staring vacantly at the rain and listening to the sound of the wind outside. Somebody pushed the door and the wind came gushing in, bringing the chill with it. I got up hastily, went to the counter to pay for my coffee and the toast, gathered my raincoat from the stand and stepped out of the café. When I looked around, there was no sign of Emma and the party.

The next I ran into Emma was when I was returning home after a tiring day. She was in her school-uniform and Charles was tagging along. I was not sure if she would care to stop and speak, but Charles, who noticed me before her, gave a tug at her skirt and pointed towards me. She stopped. Charles was looking at her eagerly. He then offered to shake hands with me in the most suave manner. I was not amused by the civil manners he put on for the sake of starting a friendship with me. A bit of sadness came over me as I looked into his eyes. In that fraction of a moment, I saw a pleading look in those eyes. It touched me somewhere. I glanced at Emma quickly. Her eyes radiated a surprise. I pulled Charles towards me and said, "What did one wall say to the other wall?" Charles looked annoyed. He turned his face away from me in an embarrassment, because this time he wanted me to take him seriously. He pressed his foot hard on my toes. I winced and said, "Ouch!" Emma quickly pulled Charles towards her and apologized on his behalf. In that struggle Charles tried to press his foot harder on my toes and finally as he stepped off my foot he stood away from me regarding me with white-hot dignity.

Emma did not try to conceal her embarrassment and anger as she pulled him further away. "I am sorry; he got furious. He has a violent temper." In the meanwhile, Charles had stationed himself securely behind Emma and continued to look at me keenly. He was clearly apprehensive and worried that he had lost a friend. But that fugitive, pleading look I had seen in his eyes before I had unwittingly offended him, had vanished. In its place, there was despair. In his small world it could hurt and I knew how it hurts. I did not let him know it and turned my attention to Emma. She was full of regret and confusion.

I was overcome by a certain sadness and loneliness as they stood before me as if asking me not to leave them so soon. I looked at the sky which showed signs of a quick drizzle which might begin any moment. The café where we had chanced to meet the other day was close by. I looked at Emma and asked her if she would care for a cup of coffee as it would warm up Charles who seemed to be shivering.

As we sat at the table with our coffee-mugs, I looked over at Charles who had started to drink his coffee using both his hands on the mug, staunchly refusing to look at me. Emma said all of a sudden, "My mother had a tendency to spoil him. My father was always careful to see that we didn't get spoilt by her indulgence; he was especially careful about Charles." She said it almost in a whisper. I looked at both of them carefully. A deep shadow had come over them as she said this. I didn't know what to say.

By now I could guess Emma fairly well; she would have spurned any demonstration of kindliness and sympathy from me.

After a brief moment of silence Emma and I looked at each other. She said, "We lost our father when Charles was barely three years of age. My mother died of grief soon after." I continued to stare at her as she sat there facing me with the look of a sad, grown-up person who was learning to take the rough and tumble of life in her stride, while her brother sat in front of us sipping at his coffee indifferently.

I could see from her demeanour that she had referred to the sad episode of their life rather inadvertently and perhaps, if Charles had not made that unusual display of temper, she wouldn't have mentioned it.

I fumbled for words, but just managed to say, "Oh, I am sorry to hear that!" Emma gave me a hearty smile like a seasoned soldier, as if to say, "Come on now that you know it, let's get on with life." But that did not help me in overcoming my uneasiness in the presence of such overwhelming fortitude. I said, looking at Charles, "Perhaps we had better not talk about this." Emma understood my meaning. She said, looking at Charles from the corner of her eye, "He is used to people referring to it. He has just begun to understand that we are different from other children. That lady who was with us the other day in the café after the singing session was over—she is our aunt who looks after us now. Charles still remembers our mother and he fights her off vehemently as if she is responsible for taking him forcibly away from his mother."

I was still wondering about how the tragedy struck this angelic pair of brother and sister when I noticed Emma fidgeting with a rather heavy-looking watch on her slender wrist. It looked very odd on her wrist because it was the kind of watch I generally noticed on the wrists of army-personnel.

I was extremely tired on that day, but I realized that for Emma and Charles, this chance meeting of ours was something like an oasis. They seemed to cherish these moments of contact. My being a stranger did not hinder the closeness they had begun to feel for me by now. Charles had finished his coffee, but unlike in our last meeting, he was not fidgety and troublesome now. He was not eager to go home. I saw him prodding his sister about something. Emma understood it and looked at him and me in amusement. "He wants to share something with you. It is something we are not allowed to look at when we are at home. So he carries it secretly in his schoolbag." I was a bit alarmed as I heard her say this. I saw Charles looking at me eagerly and Emma looking at him and smiling indulgently. I was wary. I said haltingly, "Umm, well, I hope it's nothing out of the way." Emma's expression changed rapidly from amusement and indulgence to a deep hurt. There were tears in her eyes. I was afraid she might just get up and leave. I ignored her tears and covered up my lack of tact by leaning across the table and reaching out to Charles with a great display of joviality and said, "Oh yeah! Charles, what is the secret you want to share with me?" Charles, who was blissfully unaware of the tense moment between me and his sister, fished out something from the deep pocket of his schoolbag and spread it out before me. It was a black and white photograph of a man in the army uniform. The man was full of health and energy and smiled across to the camera with the joy of life shining in every feature of his remarkably handsome face. When I looked at Charles leaning across the table, watching me proudly, there was no need for me to guess further. I looked at Emma remorsefully. She had mastered the tears, but she was in no mood to talk to me now.

I said, "Is this your father?" She just nodded. I obviously could not expect her to say more than this. I could not show any further curiosity than what was proper at that moment.

After some moments of silence I ventured to say, "But you should be proud of this photo you have of your father. Why do you have to hide it in Charles's schoolbag? Is this the only photo you have of your father?"

Emma said, "No, we have an album full of photos. But our aunt has taken it away from us. This, we had found left behind in my mother's drawer. My aunt says that children like us should not get stuck in the past, we have a long way to go, she says, and we must look ahead."

I failed to understand this piece of wisdom on the part of her aunt, but Emma seemed to have no problem with that.

I looked at Charles. The little guy, though as yet unaware of the need for self-definition and self-determination in the adult world of contradictions and strife was quietly busy folding up the sheet of brown-paper in which he had wrapped up that precious image. I did not know how to relate with the two of them who, it was quite clear to me now, were in need of me. Though I sat there facing them at that moment, a chasm of continents and culture separated me from them. I did not know if Emma was aware of this.

"How was your day at school today? Do you get to practise your choir lessons or piano lessons?" I asked to keep her mind away from the past. She looked at me despondently. Then brushing off the gloom, she said with a smile, "I haven't been able to make much progress with piano. I have neither the money nor the time for that."

I had not been watching her carefully after she said this. I was lost in the memory of my own home and family for a while. But when I looked up I found her looking at me with a sort of adult curiosity. I wondered secretly if she knew I was getting a bit drawn to her. I was quickly on my guard lest I betray any such sign of slightest involvement on my part. I folded my hands across my chest and bore an expression of detachment. She asked rather abruptly, "Do you write?" I said, pretending not to have understood her meaning, "Write? Write what?" She said, "Oh, I mean...Are you a poet or a writer—of some sort?" I tried to look offended somewhat at that and said, "Some sort? Oh, do I look 'some sort' whatever?"

She gathered herself defensively and said, "Well I just thought so." I said, "What gave you that impression?" That was a difficult question for her to answer. She reflected for a moment and said, "Perhaps there was something...well, something that appealed to my..." At that point I saw her almost swallow the word 'heart' as she paused there in embarrassment. She continued and said in completion, "To my...imagination."

I said, "I am not a practiced writer. Well I mean that's not my field really". I was actually staring at the coffee-mug in her hand. The coffee-shop where we were sitting was decent but not so well looked after, it seemed. There was a small crack showing on the otherwise beautifully crafted mug and in that despondent moment it seemed to open up a lane of memories leading me down to the boyhood days. I remembered the day when it was raining in torrents back in India on the day I was to embark on my career as a navy- cadet, my journey from home to the railway-station, my parents accompanying me, my mother silent, and my father looking after the details of my journey in a cool, business-like manner, hiding behind his stony exterior those days of admonishment, acerbic criticism and his constant effort to instil a stoic fortitude into my irresponsible adolescent days. But on that day he had hugged me tightly and in that embrace he seemed to pass on all the sorrow of his life's wisdom to me. My mother had hugged me ever so lightly because she was engaged in fighting off her tears.

All that seemed so long ago as we were sitting there in the coffee-shop. Did I ever write? Did I write about all this to anyone ever? Well, what was there to write about it anyway?

I found Emma staring at me and watching patiently. I realized that I had not answered her question yet. She was a bit scared, looking at my grim silence. I smiled in an attempt not to look as grim as that.

She said, "Oh, Perhaps I should not be so curious. I really don't realize when I start intruding on people's privacy. But that happens only when I begin to like a person, you know!' Then she immediately went on, "But I feel you must write; I don't know why I feel so; but you will write wonderfully well." I laughed. I said, "What do you think I am? A music maestro or a song-writer? I wish I was one. Then I would have written lots and lots of lyrics and set them to music for you."

"And then we would have made lots and lots of money too!" She completed the fantasy. Then she looked at me with her peculiar penetrating gaze and said, "You seem to be dreaming a lot. I saw that while we were sitting opposite you in the coffee-shop. Of course, Charles and I didn't know you then." I found it interesting how she would include Charles in all her fantastic thoughts about me. The phase of childhood which linked her closely with Charles was not yet over. She seemed to be eager however, to probe the secrets of the life of the mind and heart; she was certainly poised at that curious stage. Anyway, so long as she was not curious about my profession I was not inclined to tell her that it was far from a poetic one and as marine engineer on a naval ship my job was to handle machinery and not imagination. Besides, I could not forget that a moment ago I had hurt her by completely misapprehending the situation when they were eager to share the most precious thing in their possession and that too in the complete innocence of childhood and there she was: this young girl, responding to and encouraging a stranger to express what she perceived to be a creative imagination.

I said, "Dreaming is something everyone can do, but not everyone can write stuff out of dreams". As soon as I said this I remembered that she had said something about her father being a dreamer or some such thing. I asked her, "Was your father a dreamer?" She broke into a smile that was lovely to watch. She looked at me and said, "That's funny. You know, I feel that it was my mother who should have joined the military. The way she used to rule over the household and over him. But she would break down easily under stress. And yes; he used to dream a lot though he would never share his dreams. But don't you think that a soldier's profession is incompatible with dreaming?"

On a spur of the moment I said spontaneously, "No, it isn't." She looked surprised at my unguarded revelation, and looked at me, as if in need of a clarification. Then she uttered her words slowly, "Are you...a soldier?" Charles was looking at me with dilated pupils now. The mention of his father and his father being a soldier had sent waves of alertness and curiosity in him. He was suddenly out of his mood for pranks. I kept looking at the crack in the mug.

I said, "Soldiers are in need of dreaming more than anyone else."

That meeting ended on that inconclusive note. For Charles it was a vague understanding of something that teased him and waited to be found out in the image of his father which stared at him tantalizingly always; something which his sensitivity, hovering between childhood loss and the tenacious demands of life, was unable to explain to him. Emma had looked at the watch on her hand and made ready to go. Charles had followed her reluctantly, turning around to look at me a couple of times as they moved out of the coffee-shop. I expected Emma to turn around and say good-bye to me; but she didn't.

When I reached my lodging it was dark and as I switched on the light I saw the three letters which I had left there on my writing table. They were still lying there unopened.

I kicked my boots under the table, removed the woollens and took a deep breath before finally making up my mind to open the letters now. Two long letters from Neela and a brief and anxious letter from mother. Everything looked as expected. Neela was full of anxiety over my long absence and the delay in replying to her last letter. I ran over the content in a cursory glance. The last one that needed to be opened was from mother. It was terse and as always, I read between the lines. After the routine questions about my well-being she mentioned in the last line her major concern about the need of cash as an emergency requirement on account of father's hospitalization.

The first major mission before me next morning was to visit my headquarters and arrange to transfer money to hometown. I had on my hand the time of a week or so before starting on my voyage back.

I might see Emma on her way to school if I managed to plan my schedule accordingly. But I trembled at the thought. It was destined to be my last encounter with Emma and Charles.

I wasn't sure how she would take it. She was mature and level-headed. But I was not sure of myself. And most of all I felt concerned for Charles. He had just learnt to calm down after he had begun to trust me in his innocent but proud way. It would be another rather cruel stroke of destiny to be deprived of someone who had begun to figure as a father and a friend. .

That night I was left with no appetite. The night came without a sound. I prayed, solely for Emma, and Charles desolately..

That night I dreamed a dream of Emma, or rather a dream that she would have dreamed. It was a large dining table in a cool dark dining hall with an overhanging lampshade, a kind of Victorian type of house. Emma's family had gathercd around the table as if it was a long awaited reunion; Emma, and Charles, a grown up happy young man, and they wcre all sharing some tough thoughts and soft prayers. I wasn't anywhere in that dream, and yet the dream was a part of me.

That was a short but good sleep and I got up feeling hopeful and peaceful, not for me so much as vicariously for Emma.

The next day, after quickly transacting the business at the bank I looked at the watch. It was rather early to expect Emma and Charles as yet. But not to leave it to chance I decided to wait at the coffee shop. The sky was bright. It wasn't likely to rain. I took a seat close to the entrance . I ordered stuff that would keep me engaged at least for the next half an hour.

I was looking attentively at the road outside until the first batch of school children appeared on the scene.. Their laughter drifted towards me on the breeze but Emma and Charles weren't among them. The sky that was bright some time ago was now cloudy and grey. As the time passed slowly I was getting restless with anxiety. I was feeling a bit awkward also, sitting alone and having no idea as to how long I would be able to stay there idling away perhaps hours at a stretch. And I could not bury my head in a book pretending to read because my guests might pass that way and we would both miss each other. Everything seemed to be in danger of going wrong, the weather, the time, the day and my unreasonable longing to see them as if my life depended on that meeting. A chance acquaintance that happened to take place in some vacant hours, and if someone were to foresee the effect so deep I would not have given credence to it.

Another group of children was coming and the augury was made by their playful kidding and laughter. I eagerly scanned their faces but could not find Emma and Charles. I began to feel lost on the high sea now with nothing to see on the horizon. Where was I going to look for them except for this road and this coffee shop as my radar? Everything was perhaps to end as hastily and abruptly as it had begun. The flow of children walking to their school had stopped by now. I looked at the watch. I had spent half an hour already. It was not justifiable to prolong my presence at the coffee-shop beyond the next ten minutes. And if at all I chanced to meet them as I started walking back home they would be found in a tearing hurry to reach school. And did I wait here for them just to have a glimpse of them? Honestly not.

I decided to end the waiting and looked up finally, giving up my long and steady vigilant watch over the road that was to bring Emma and Charles within my sight. As I stood up feeling into my pocket for the wallet I saw the lady at the shop counter watching me with curious eyes. It seemed she had noted my two meetings with Emma and Charles earlier, and perhaps had guessed that I was waiting for them.

The girl at the counter was watching me as I started walking towards the counter, and gave me a cordial smile as I was about to pay the bill. She said politely, "I buy the coffee and the toast for you sir. The bill is on me." I looked at her with a question mark. She said, " Emma and her aunt have been my friends . I have known them for a long time. They went to school rather early today. You just missed them." To avoid any further embarrassment to me she clarified, "I was there at the counter when you last met them. Can I help sir?"

This filled me with confidence and I said, "It was a chance meeting. And I liked them. My stay in Vancouver will end shortly and I will go back to India where I come from. I would like to say hello to them before I go."

She said, " You will definitely see them if you come here again around five in the evening. That's the time when they drop by every evening."

The next day as I reached the coffee shop Emma and Charles were waiting. Emma was sitting with her back towards the door. I found Charles looking fixedly at the road . He wasn't fidgety but rather calm which was unlike Charles. He nudged Emma but she did not look in my direction. I approached their table and she got up rather deferentially. That too was unlike Emma. Both had been silently brooding over the last meeting when Emma had suddenly withdrawn and walked away with Charles in tow. I could see the sense of misgiving writ large on Charles's face. He suddenly seemed to have changed over the last two days. A misgiving crossed my mind too. Did they regret that they had let me know them more intimately than they should.

Emma broke the ice." I am sorry you waited long expecting to see us in the morning." She said tentatively to start the conversation.

I pulled a chair and positioned it between the chairs of Emma and Charles as we all sat around the table. Emma now sat down and looked at me as I fumbled for words and simultaneously tried to guess her mood. I made a feeble attempt not to look grim..

Emma understood. "Will you be leaving for India?" She asked, not suddenly but unceremoniously.

I said," Yes.. " And I glanced at Charles. His eyes dilated. He was not ready to reconcile with the idea of parting so soon.. In the meantime Emma got up quietly and went to the counter. I saw her coming back with the tray of coffee and sandwiches.

While she was at the counter I asked Charles, "Any new quiz for me today?" He fished out a sketchbook from his schoolbag. He had drawn three figures, a tall man, and the other two, a skinny girl holding a book aloft, and a boy, his mouth wide open, in a laughter perhaps, dancing, throwing his hands up. Behind them were drawn horizontal, wavy lines which was most likely the sea, and vertical lines which were like the tall masts of boats.

"What is this? I mean who are they?" I asked. "Guess", he said, looking minutely at his own creation. You have to answer", he said, giving me a challenging look. I pretended not to have understood. He said, "This is Emma and this is me."

"And who is the third figure?" I asked. And I was really puzzled. "This is the quiz. You have to answer", he said.

I pulled a blank face and said, " I give up." I knew very well that was what he wanted to hear. He pouted his mouth and nodded his head up and down. Then looked at me and giggled. Then said triumphantly, " That is you!".

Just then Emma reached the table and before putting the tray down she peered over Charles's shoulder to look at our object of interest. I looked at her to read her expression. A thin smile flitted across her face. She put the tray down and settled in her chair facing me and Charles.

She was trying to hide the pain over Charles's innocent and trustful involvement in me. For no fault of mine I feared there was a subtle resentment in that expression. After a brief moment of silence we were about to speak simultaneously and both stopped to give the other the chance. I expected her to speak about my date of departure, the impending doomsday as it were. But Emma's astute mind decided to elude the obvious. Skipping the expected she said, " How are you placed tomorrow morning? Tomorrow is Sunday. Charles and I would like to spend it with you if your time permits!"

I said, "I have absolutely no problem. But will your aunt permit you to go out with a stranger that I am?"

Emma said without hesitation, " I'll manage." And with that she looked at Charles. They both seemed to be like a duo who were used to working in collusion over finding a way out in such situations.

The next morning we were three of us at Jericho beach facing the Pacific. The sky was changing the moods fast. I hoped it would not rain like the day on our first meeting. But soon the clouds dispersed and the sunshine was clear and falling straight and candid over the sea.

Emma and Charles had come prepared to spend long hours of that Sunday on the beach with me. There was the breath of freedom in their presence, the way they were dancing to the rhythm of some song that Emma had picked up recently from her music lessons. Charles threw his hands up in the air like the child he had drawn in the sketchbook. This went on for some time until Charles found a mound of a sandcastle somebody had started making and left half way, incomplete. He got busy building it up again in his own way.

Looking at Charles who was busy meticulously shaping the form of the new castle, Emma looked pensive. I asked her about her unexplained and abrupt exit of that day. She did not speak for some time but the pause did not last long. Without turning to look at me she said, "I cannot quite explain and you will not understand. It had to do with the loss we suffered over our father's death. My parents were deeply attached to each other. My mother who was outwardly a strong person was not all that strong really. She was dependent on my father in many ways. Financially we were secured but that was not the point. In spite of her brave effort to get on with life and with her devotion and duty as mother she had caved in and collapsed under the stress. When you mentioned you being from the armed forces I recalled all that we had gone through." She paused.

I did not ask her anything more. The Pacific ocean was deep and the wind had stopped. The yachts parked in the distance were softly swaying and the masts drew lines against the deep blue sky. Emma had taken the burden off her chest. Perhaps she needed to do it earlier but could not Sometimes someone who is relatively a stranger like me is the safest outlet to relieve such stressful moments.

Emma did not know how to resume the conversation. She was keeping distance out of the awareness that there was no more meeting again, and Charles being aware of Emma's intermittent silence during the conversation was feeling something amiss. Between my first chance encounter with them after her practice session and now, both Emma and Charles had taken on a different note. The absence of parents in their life had caused a rupture that was difficult to overcome yet. They seemed to be living constantly in fear of some invisible third eye ready to admonish them for some lapses in their conduct.

I longed to comfort them and instil in them a confidence that would help them the entire lifetime to come. I had sensed that confidence in Emma the very first time I saw her glancing at the audience casually during that practice session in her quiet certainty that she would excel if she found an opportunity. It warmed my heart to see that there was no waywardness in either of them. Both knew very early in life that they had to be their own angels. I was myself feeling small in the presence of such fortitude.

Charles was fed up of playing by himself. He had given up the castle and was now playing with some new acquaintance. Surprisingly, Charles was not up to his dangerous games and the two were getting along well until the other boy responded to the call of his mother and was ready to go. Looking at Charles so despondent, the boy's mother came to them with a cordial smile and said a few words to Charles. She seemingly promised Charles and her son that they would both be able to play together the next Sunday. Charles responded pleasantly and my heart was at peace seeing that Charles was not without people who understood children's needs and were quick to respond without any overt display of kindness.

I asked Emma if she knew that lady. Emma said she knew the family was originally from Greece and had just recently come to stay in the neighbourhood. She said that Charles seemed to have liked the boy and got on rather well with him.. By now all three of us were hungry and Emma unpacked the sandwiches to share.

After the sandwiches we decided to walk to the end of the beach towards the jetty. The sun was mild and there were no signs of rain. The Pacific ocean was calm and pleasant.

Jericho beach, the Jericho Park, and the Pacific ocean were full of blessings for the three of us on that day of sunshine. For Emma and Charles it was a day of freedom in the presence of the Pacific ocean, and for me who was spending most of the days on sea, it was a day in the presence of the warmth of earth. They were invited to dream of the future and I who recalled my days of apprenticeship, was recalling the time of thrill and fear when our submarine was passing under the sea and there was no sign of humanity anywhere.

There was no despondency anywhere near. I rejoiced at the sight of Charles frolicking around and Emma, assured, at peace with herself and her world. We were together, yet apart, each cocooned in one's given world, and yet connected with a magnetic thread. We sat down on a bench under an oak tree while Charles left to chase a black rabbit he had spotted in the weeds. Emma looked at me. I knew by now that such long stretches of silence were not to her taste. Especially when we knew our time was limited, silence was a dreadful waste of time for her. I was a precious entity for her and Charles; some one through whom they wanted to know more about the life and the world they were waiting to embark upon.

Like a vessel drifting along a ripple of thought she asked me, "What is it like when you are on the sea?"

I said, "Being an engineer, I have to be in the engine room most of the time. But the hours I spent on the deck watching the sea were many. Bewitching to say the least. Sometimes the vastness and and the endless time and space filled with nothing else but the sky and the sea is awful."

Emma said, " I have never been out of sight of the shore, never been that deep into the sea. I have always watched the sea from the shore."

I said, "My first lesson in life was to overcome the fear of the sea. It was not easy. Our ship was caught in an awesome storm when crossing the Suez Canal. We were all cadets then. We were sick like anything, more out of fear than physical distress. We longed to get out of it all and quit this hazardous profession. After that I kept in mind the words of Christopher Columbus which I had read somewhere in a school book: "You never cross the ocean until you lose sight of the shore."

Emma was looking wistfully at the tranquil sea. She was trying to figure out something. But I did not intrude. She wasn't looking at me because we were both looking in the same direction, the sea. By this time, Charles who was tired of his solitary games had come back and joined us. He sat next to Emma, eager to listen.

Emma said, Did you know you were making a hard decision when you joined the Navy?"

I said, " I had read a small introductory book on Indian Navy when I was in school. I was a different guy before reading that book". I looked at Charles. He was looking expectantly at me. I could read the question which said, "Like me?" I looked back and said, "Yes; I was like you, a prankster!"

Charles snuggled close to his sister. He was all ears now. Emma said, "Tell him all about you as a cadet."

I said, "Well, It is a rather long story. My basic training was in Chilka in Orissa.. There I was trained for six months to learn the basic rules and discipline.. That was a beginning of change in me."

The story of "a change in me" drew the attention of Charles more than of Emma. He got up from Emma's side and boldly snuggled up to me. Emma too looked at me intently.

I said, "After a period of six months, staying away from family, I was granted a month's leave to visit home. After that we would not be able to see our land and people for a long time. I wanted to thoroughly enjoy every minute of that month. But in the midst of it all, a feeling arose that I was different now, and had to be different, from the rest of friends. I was a soldier first and all other relationships had a subordinate place thereafter in my life."

I paused for a look at Emma. She and Charles were getting what they needed to know, an insight into the inner man that their father was. By now our conversation was going along the track of intuition.

The day I had my first glimpse of the life of Emma and Charles in the coffee shop I never thought I would be drawn to them with a strong magnetic pull, and that in a few chance meetings they would seek a soul-mate in a stranger like me. It was a small tryst with destiny.

I took up the loose strands of the conversation and continued. "I still remember the day my parents came to the Railway station to see me off to my next phase of three month's training to Cochin in Kerala. That day I was upset again as I was leaving my parents for a long time. That day the rain was in full swing.. It was heavily raining. The train started and after more than 2 days I arrived at Cochin. I was shocked when I came to know that the people there didn't know Hindi.. But I managed one taxi driver to drop me at the naval base..... After that I reported on board my ship.. It was the first time I was looking at such a big ship in my life.. It was like a mini city.. Next day my shipmate introduced me to other trainees who were going to accompany us. It took me almost 10 days to adjust myself to the conditions of the ship. After that our ship went to Goa, followed by our scheduled visits to foreign countries like Italy and Egypt. During our voyage the sea was normal but when we arrived at Suez Canal at Mediterranean Sea the sea had gone worst like hell. The sea was very rough and our ship was rolling and pitching. We were scared like small kids and praying for our lives to god. For that whole night we were scared.. But next day in the afternoon the sea was calm and silent like a river."

I paused. I was introspecting. My days on the ship, and the ensnarement of the sea, the bewitching goddess and her many moods! Stunning, awesome, vast! Once she claims you, she claims you forever! Her sounds, her calm, and her fury! The truth of my life, and who knows, perhaps of my death!

The sun had begun to decline. The Pacific ocean was sending signals to the yachts and the birds to return. The sea gulls were crossing the sea. It was a time of longing for something innate to the sea; the waves and the rocks, and the horizon. Something vast was taking on a form of something I could see. A cosmic tide of a feeling moved and touched the sky, and a scattered mass of cloud was dissipating fast in the vaults of the sky, and in its dissipation it portrayed a magnanimous love happening across the sky.

I could feel a calm descending upon all three of us. That hour and those moments had touched the three living creatures with the spirit of the magnanimity of the sea and each was trying to read its endless script in different ways.

It was time to go. Emma and Charles had to reach home before dark and I had to go to my Highbury apartment and gather my scattered spirits.

I looked at both of them. Charles who was sitting next to me had got up first and was dusting off the sand particles hugging his jacket and hair. Emma looked at him with amusement. She was familiar with his ways and the mind. His resilience was his chief strength. And perhaps he was her mentor in some respects, though she was his elder sister. She stood up; took a deep breath, and smiled at me. In that smile, I found an assurance that she was the same Emma I had seen at the practice session, one among the many children, on the threshold of youth, and ready with a casual awareness of her difference from other children, a precocious girl-child who was taught early by life to carry herself with insouciance.

My mind was at peace.

The next three days were extremely busy for me as my attention was divided over many things under the focus. I hardly had any time to think of myself. In between, I thought of Emma and Charles intermittently, but avoided the temptation of seeing them again. I was busy with the correspondence with my headquarters at India. When at last everything was in order I thought of strolling along the paths I had trodden, mornings, evenings and sometimes at night but wasn't sure if I would be able to do it again without feeling the wrench in my heart.

I could imagine Emma and Charles walking past the coffee-shop, morning and evening, glancing at the place I had waited for them to see them walk in, soaked in rain. Then on one such night I prayed for them as never before, intensely, passionately, devoutly. I remembered the instructions their aunt had given them not to get entangled in any emotional ties lest they lose focus on their goals in life. There was truth in the lady's advice however harsh it sounded to me when I heard it first from Emma. I respected the lady for her perspective on life.

I convinced myself that another meeting was neither likely nor desirable. But it was not in place to leave them without a word of final good bye. After a lot of procrastination I decided to write a small note of thanks addressed to both. I am poor at expressing feelings in writings or gestures. I feel myself hollow and superfluous when I try to do that. I knew the safest and the surest channel to deliver the note into their hands was through the girl at the counter who had read my mind last time and helped me.

The next morning as I was relatively free, I decided to proceed towards the coffee shop taking care to avoid the time when Emma and Charles would be passing that way to school. I knew a florist on that way at the next corner on Alma street. I collected a few daisies and chrysanthemum and asked the florist to make a bouquet. Then I suddenly remembered the girl at the counter who had read my mind and played a role in arranging my meeting with Emma and Charles. I hurriedly asked the florist girl to make one more. She made the two bouquets and handed them to me with a graceful smile which was characteristic of the people living in Vancouver.. I took it with thanks, the first ever, and the last bouquet I had bought for some while living in Vancouver.

As I hurriedly barged into the coffee-shop the girl at the counter noticed me with a look of surprise, seeing me walk in with the two bouquets in my hand. I explained to her who the bouquets were meant for and she smiled. I told her that I would be leaving for India and there were only two days left before my departure, and that I would not be able to meet Emma and Charles again. She thanked me for the bouquets and promised to deliver Emma's bouquet and the note as soon as she met Emma next. I was about to leave the shop when it struck me that I was leaving Emma clueless about my whereabouts in case she wanted to contact me in future. I turned around and handed my business cards to the girl, one for Emma and one for her to keep.

On the appointed day I embarked upon my voyage back to India.

The brief episode ended, but not without an indelible mark in my memory. The ocean would be silent at night and I would spend a few hours watching the journey of the moon and the stars from the deck wondering about the mystery of human bondage.

Years passed by. I rose to a higher rank in the next few years. Life was full of excitement and new challenges but the memory of Emma and Charles accompanied me at every stage. In the coming years I was blessed with two kids and my parents spent the last few years of their life in contentment.

One day, as I returned home as I was off duty on account of my three months leave, my wife gave me a letter and a small parcel. The letter had travelled a long distance as it had an inaccurate address written on it. The handwriting on the envelope was neat and elegant.

The letter was pasted and securely tied to the parcel. I weighed the parcel curiously as I simultaneously felt a strange vibration coming from the parcel.

I opened the parcel and to my surprise the letter and the parcel were from Emma.

I took a long pause before opening it, not being able to make up my mind whether to open the letter or the parcel first. I was flooded with memories of Vancouver and Emma.

The parcel first! I gently removed the wrapping. There was a wristwatch inside, the same wristwatch which I had seen on Emma's wrist on our first meeting on that rainy day in the coffee shop. I scanned the letter, hastily at a glance and then slowly again to imbibe every word. Nearly twelve years had elapsed after that day.

She wrote, "Dear Mr. Pratap Sharma, I do not know where to begin. There is a huge time lapse. I am not sure if you will remember the Emma you had met on a rainy day in Vancouver. For me and Charles you are the same precious soul without a name. It was painful for me that you did not spare a few minutes to hand over that bouquet to me personally. We missed you terribly, especially Charles. Anyway. We valued your company. You left a deep mark on us in that short period. Certain things happen in life and bring about a change.

To come back to the present... Charles has changed a lot. He is a responsible young man with a lot of understanding and patience. You were his role model after that day we spent on the beach as he listened intently to you describing your experience of the sea. He is a cadet now in the Canadian national cadet corps and will soon be a part of the naval force. I am getting engaged to Kevin Walsh, my friend from our school days.

He teaches music and piano in a college academy in Vancouver. I shall soon take up a job in the same college.

You must be puzzled over the watch. It is the same watch you used to look at with a question in your eyes. It belonged to my father. I wanted to find a rightful place for that watch and I thought of you. It belongs to you. It will have its rightful place on your wrist. Please accept it.

There was no formal ending at the end of the letter.

I stared at the watch as I wore it on my wrist respecting Emma's wish, and it has become a part of my life thereafter.

That is Emma, forever ago.

The End.

BLACK IS BEAUTIFUL

This is a story of a lovely black girl from an obscure village of Tanzania. Since I've forgotten the names of both: I mean, the name of the girl as well as the village, because they both belong to that 'once upon a time' slot of all traditional stories, let us give them names. The girl was Ulla and the village was Zincoba. Actually, Ulla is the name of a lovely Chinese flower, and that's so much the better for our story because our black girl was as lovely as a flower. She carried the fragrance of her girlhood blossoming into youth all around her. Looking at her none felt the need to be reminded that 'black is beautiful' because she was both black and beautiful.

But Ulla lived in a strange world. She got up to the shrill, cantankerous shouting of her mother, aunts and granny. Then her rowdy brothers got up, and if she dared to sleep longer, ignoring all the hell around her, one of them would come to her and kick her with a great gusto: ha ha! That would kick Ulla out of her dreams too!

The mornings used to be occupied by all the concerted noises made by all the women of the household and her three brothers who were devil incarnate. "Ulla this,

37

Ulla that, where is Ulla? Ulla, can't you hear?" And that would keep Ulla on her toes throughout the morning. In the afternoon her rowdy brothers would return from the farm, hungry as wolves, kick their muddy shoes around, and slapping her hard on the back with their muddy hands, would rush to hog their meals.

After the meals the men folks would rush to grab the most comfortable and cosy nook of the house for the luxury of their afternoon nap while Ulla would sit down to share meals with the women of the household.
Those were the days when the women of the household and those of the neighbourhood had started looking at her grown up body with a critical interest. She was a commodity to be disposed of now, the stronger the girl, the better the deal; and yes, the sooner, the better!

Ulla understood the look in their eyes. She was filled with horror because soon she would have to show everyone that she was strong enough to withstand the ordeals of that thing called marriage which would bring into her life a monster called 'husband', who she knew, would be as awful as her brothers, if not worse.

One day her mother called her for a task, which actually turned out to be a very neurotic session of the mission 'educating Ulla'. When she entered her mother's room, she found her mother surrounded by a number of wiseacre women of the neighbourhood. When she went in, they looked her up and down, as if she was a mare on sale. There was a look of great pity in their eyes which filled her mother with an unwarranted inferiority complex. Actually they were struck by Ulla's charm which none of them possessed. But neither Ulla nor her dense mother could see through their mask which concealed their envy.

Her mother stupidly went on endorsing all their wicked comments and evaluations of Ulla and Ulla listened open-mouthed to their glib talk about how a girl should dress and conduct herself. Ulla looked all the more ungainly in spite of her clean, glossy black complexion and slender waist. The women were mighty pleased with themselves as their comments made Ulla's mother crestfallen and made Ulla confirmed in her belief that she was no good like that ugly duckling of Hans Andersen's story.

The result of that frenetic half-an-hour session of 'educating' Ulla was that her mother was thoroughly demoralized for having given birth to a daughter who was good for nothing. Her frustration, as it became more and more visible and audible, heightened the morale of the women and they rejoiced over their success as Ulla looked pathetic. She cut a sorry figure indeed, among all those worldly wise Dianas of this earth.

After the women had left (but not before extracting a good ransom in terms of tea and snacks, with an implicit promise not to visit them again till the next fortnight or two) Ulla's mother dragged her to the backyard and said, "You are grown up now; but look at your waist, thin as a wisp. You will break down after the first kick, and then, no husband for you. Here, go and fetch water from the river. And remember; you are not going to stop before you complete three rounds. At your age, we used to fetch water, grind millet for ten people, and work from dawn to dusk."

Ulla understood; but you may not understand. What the hell is the link between a kick and a husband? Well, in that village in Tanzania, it was required of girls to show that they could withstand kicking from their husbands. The girl would be made to sit firmly on a rock and the boy would come from behind, running like a fast bowler in a cricket-match and kick the girl in the waist with all the force he could muster. The girl should neither fall off nor cry. Then the boy had no way but to marry her. Of course, you can imagine how the boys would bend the rules to suit their choice. But Ulla's mother and Ulla were not too hopeful of coming across a smart Alec who would eat his cake and have it too! Besides, most of the boys and men were too vain and thoroughly unromantic to make any concessions even to the most beautiful of the girls.

So that's how it was for Ulla. The formula had set in her mind: one kick, no fall is equal to marriage is equal to husband.

But what was a husband equal to? There was a big question mark.

She wanted to ask her mother how many times she fell off the rock or cried in pain. Then she explained to herself: perhaps father did not kick mother hard enough; or did he? Can't one marry without that great kick?

Every now and then Ulla would sit quietly to find a solution. In those days, her friends were full of stories. One of them told her how a certain boy had caught a glimpse of the girl whom he was going to kick and had fallen for her. When his parents noticed it they were furious and warned him not to perform the kicking half-heartedly. If he did, God would be angry and would not bless the marriage. No God blesses a marriage based on dishonesty, they said. They said that both the boy and the girl must face the test without cheating on the rules. So the poor boy kicked really hard and the girl fell off the rock, and the boy ran to her in panic to pick her up. But alas, they were too honest, and so the boy could not marry the girl. He ended up marrying an amazon of a girl;

but that's another story.

Ulla had laughed to death when she heard that story. But now as the destined hour was approaching fast, she lost her laughter and even her smiles. She looked grave.

Then started the ordeal of preparing Ulla for the test. Her mother was anxious that her daughter should pass the test in the first go. She herself had failed five times; so much so that her parents had lost hope of ever getting her married. She now blamed it on her parents because they had not prepared her adequately for the test, she said.

Then one day, the family sat together to discuss the matter and they decided unanimously to train Ulla properly for the test. Henceforth everyone in the family, even Ulla's younger brother, would kick Ulla hard, at least thrice a day. "And no mercy, mind you," said Ulla's granny sternly. The boys laughed gleefully. They were already in the habit of doing it; but now they could do it with an official sanction.

"Ho, ho, Ulla," they would say, "We are going to find the best of guys for you; don't worry. But a good one doesn't come along without a price." And everyone agreed on this last piece of wisdom.

So day in and day out, with every summons from anyone of the family, Ulla had to press her teeth and face a hard one, and that too without a protest.

Ulla started wondering what was really going on. Were they simply using her as a punching bag to vent their anger for some reason? Or had they really found someone whom they were keen to make their son-in-law? There was nothing she could do but to wait and watch.

One day she lost her patience and turned around, and gave a good bashing up to her brother. His wailing brought everyone there and they were delirious with joy, as if they had heard the wailing of a new-born babe. Ulla's feat deserved kudos according to them, not because her brother was a bully and deserved to get such a bashing up anyway, but because "Our darling Ulla can now pass the test in the first attempt," they said.

Ulla was at a loss to make any sense out of this. "For God's sake, put an end to this vaudeville and the absurd preliminaries. Show the bloody horse to me once and for all and I'll know what to do. But let me see that cursed guy first!" she said once.

Everyone was alarmed and alerted at once, as if they had heard some blasphemy from her mouth. Her mother said, "Holy one, you are not to say such inauspicious things before your marriage. And another thing, more important: under no circumstances are you going to see the boy, nor is he going to catch a glimpse of you! Oh Lord, we know what tricks the boys and girls of this generation pick up from one another. In our times... " And blah blah blah, she went on to say things which every new generation is bound to hear from the older one.

One day, Ulla was standing in the backyard watching a man loading a donkey with sacks of cotton. The donkey had been tolerant enough to bear the burden up to a point. But suddenly the wise one (the donkey) lost his (or was it she?) temper and kicked his master hard with his hind legs. It happened so suddenly and unexpectedly that the man fell flat on his back. The sight filled Ulla with such joy that she laughed to her heart's content as never before.

In another household, a little further down, another scene was unfolding. Let's call the guy Gwana, because anyway, we have to give him a name, though we need not be fussy about it. A man with any name will sound nasty all the same, and he has to, you know! What's there in a (man's) name?

It was time to find a bride for Gwana. Gwana was alright, I mean, he was strong, dark, tall, and all that, but oh, he was not rowdy, not a rascal, not a rogue; in fact, he was without all those abstract, intangible virtues expected in a boy of his age.

He was being given a 'talking to' by his father who was advising him, mind you, not admonishing! He was told how a boy of his age must thrive in the presence of someone who inspired fear, like for example, his own father, or better still, his grandfather. The girls should not be foolish enough to seek his attention but stand away in awe; they should not perceive him as their protector, but had better regard him as a threat to their very existence if they dared to disregard or disobey him. Gwana put on a deadpan face and pretended to listen obediently.

Actually he was nervous at the prospect of having to run, and then after that really vigorous start, go and kick the woman hard in her waist; that too in front of all the curious spectators! And what, if in spite of a good start, he lost nerve at the critical moment and failed to deliver the goods? What if that stupid nanny, instead of falling off, turned around and showed all her thirty two teeth to him in a wicked 'hee hee' of a triumph? In fact he was advised by one of his sagacious friends not to spare any of them, and go and kick them so hard that would knock the daylight out of their brains, because whoever they were, "As a rule, all of them deserve to be kicked anyway. Don't expect them to be angels, you know! Especially the one who is going to withstand the kick is surely not going to be an angel," he had said with the bright light of wisdom in his eyes.

"But then where would the angel be? Most likely to be among those who fall off!" Gwana had asked in a dilemma.

"The simple bait is not to marry, my dear friend. Because the rules are such that you are unlikely to marry an angel and the one you are likely to end up marrying is going to be far from an angel!" His friend had summed up the whole thing very wisely. But it left Gwana in a fix.

What do you think, my friends? After all, Gwana and Ulla were not a pair of star-crossed lovers like Romeo and Juliet. At this stage, we can't even say, like cock-sure philistines that marriages are made in heaven. If not Ulla and Gwana, then some other pair, until some of them hit it off, no matter who they are: any xyz and Ulla, or any xyz and Gwana, or who knows, Gwana and Ulla after all! Besides, Gwana did not know whether Ulla was an angel nor did Ulla know whether Gwana or that 'bloody horse', if you may put it that way, was indeed a guy whose kick was worth a goldmine.

I know, you are dying to know what happened next. But that after a little break! And by now, I must have left you guessing as to who I am: a hard-core feminist or a die-hard macho! Keep guessing. The answer is not hard to find.

Hello everybody; we are meeting after a long break; thanks for bearing with me.

The doomsday arrived. There was no need to get Ulla dressed up for the occasion; that could wait for another day. Gwana had a confidential talk with his sagacious friend before setting out on his mission of choosing the right one whom he was going to wed. Ulla had no such privilege; she had to trust her own instinct and luck; the latter was going to be more decisive than the former.

Somehow, Gwana's aunt had come to know that Ulla was a delicate darling. She observed Gwana carefully to see if he too had got to know it. She was satisfied to see no such sign but still, to make doubly sure, she spoke loudly for everyone to hear, "Gwana will have to do his best; otherwise he will bring shame upon the family; the girl is quite sturdy."

Gwana made his calculations: a sturdy girl; will need a hard knock. If she doesn't fall, Gwana marries her. His friend gave him a knowing look. Gwana secretly sneaked inside to test his muscle-power.

His aunt however, had other plans. She had seen Gwana and his friend exchange a look. She smirked complacently. She knew how Gwana's mind worked. Now Gwana will knock off Ulla and there will be a good chance to get him to marry her own niece.

Gwana set out, accompanied by his family, and of course, by his sagacious friend. He was nervous like a a warrior who was going to shoot in the dark.

When they reached Ulla's house they were taken straight to the battleground, because it was not a custom among them to stand on ceremony on such occasions; they meant business!

Far from the spot from where Gwana was going to take a start, Ulla was sitting on a rock with her back turned on the spectators, gazing blankly in front of her.

But just before the ritual was to start, and before Gwana could afford a glimpse of Ulla from the rear, his aunt came running to him and pushed him out of view. She told him to wait and as everybody watched, wondering what she was up to, she rushed to Ulla's mother uproariously and admonished her for making Ulla's slender waist all too noticeable. Ulla's mother was hurt and furious. In fact, she was following the rules honestly. Besides, she was a simple soul, incapable of any trickery.

In that hullaballoo, Ulla turned, and lo! The first one to set his eyes upon her was none else but Gwana. Their eyes met for a fraction of a second, and before anyone knew, Ulla turned her back on the scene, and sat as before, staring ahead blankly. But she had liked what she saw in that fraction of a second.

But now she feared the test. She had seen Gwana flexing his muscles in readiness, all set to deliver the great kick. Ulla recalled her rigorous training of the past one month and braced herself for the fateful blow.

That moment came. Ulla pressed her teeth together so hard that she bit her own lips. She was determined not to fall off the rock.

Gwana's sagacious friend patted him on the back and reminded him to do his best, to put all the power in the punch and give a hard knock to the adversary sitting in front of him. Gwana nodded as he took a start.

Ulla waited breathlessly for the great knock-off! And good lord, it was a gentle knock, as if somebody had gently tapped on the door.

Gwana stopped, breathless with excitement and more out of nervousness. Ulla was there before his eyes, still sitting on the rock. He did not know if it was his nervousness that did the trick.

Ulla's family was delirious with triumph. They all rallied around Ulla, everybody taking the credit for giving a real hard lesson to Ulla in the course of her training.

Gwana's aunt was left wondering how this wisp of a girl could withstand the knock. She kept looking at Ulla's slender waist; nothing had changed; Ulla's waist was as slender as ever.

And so, my friends, Gwana married Ulla in the midst of all the hassle over dowry and the scenes made by his bad-tempered aunt.

What happened thereafter? I do not know. But let's hope, they lived happily thereafter, forever.

The Homecoming

Nachiketa is a character from Kathopanishad.

There is a dialogue between this young boy and Yama—the divinity of Death in the Indian mythology.

Long back, this boy had captured my imagination and I framed him in a narrative that took its flight from the basic ground in the Upanishad and then made its own flight-path.

I had shoved it under a pile of old files. I remembered it and decided to release it. Two persons had read it closely when it was written; both have departed from this world. One of them was my father and the other was my spiritual Guru. . My Guru read it and smiled. As was his custom, he never opined on anything. But he passed on the story to his trusted friend to read. I think they both liked it, because my notebook passed through quite a few hands before it came back to me through my Guru to whom I had originally given it. Here is my take on the original story in the Upanishad, with a considerable liberty of the flight of imagination.

Nachiketa stretched his supple limbs like a kitten and lay in bed a little longer, feeling the warmth of the deerskin bed. He felt its bristling soft touch pressed against his body like a fond animal. For a few moments he was on the verge of sleep and reality, undecided about what to choose. For a while his dream continued to cling to him like a warm restful kitten and then pressing itself hard against him, the dream sprang away and Nachiketa woke up but refused to open his eyes. He wanted to snuggle close to his mother. With his eyes shut, he expected to seek the warmth of her body surrounding him like a cascade of mango leaves. But when he lifted his hand it fell through the empty space surrounding him. He opened his eyes and blinked as his eyes caught the shafts of the morning sunlight descending on him through the slits in the ventilators of the cottage. He turned over and found that the space where his mother lay asleep had been vacant for a long time. It had already absorbed the morning mist and felt dewy and cold now.

Nachiketa sprang out of his bed in panic, anticipating his father's wrath. But when he came out in the courtyard, he was thrilled to tread softly on the warm, crisp floor freshly plastered with cow dung. The place was full of the aroma of ghee being poured into the sacrificial fire and the deep sound of mantras being chanted in unison. The thatched cottage wore a festive look with men and women bustling around. His father presided over all of them He looked lustrous with his broad forehead stretching back to meet the bald crown of his head making one whole radiant sphere.

Nachiketa rushed through his morning routine and then frisked away with a set of fresh clothes tucked under his arm. he went straight to the riverbed for his bath. He sat awhile on the bank resting his back against the crusty surface of a solid rock. As he sat there looking at the quiet, rippling expanse of the river, blissful lethargy caressed his limbs. He watched the shimmering ebony bodies of the buffaloes wading in the sun-kissed waters of the river.

Nachiketa had begun to hear the sound of silence these days. Whenever he watched the expanse of the river, whenever he sat here watching buffaloes and the sheer contrast of the white cranes taking a ride on the shimmering dark backs of those indolent animals, he would hear silence. He wanted to share it with his mother, but she would be too busy to accompany him on his idle excursions into wilderness. He understood silence; the silence of the wilderness, and yet it was different from the silence of his mother.

When he finished his bath and came out, he was dripping wet. He liked to splash water and sprinkle tiny beads of water on the lotus leaves in the river-bed. Yesterday he had tried to make his mother laugh by trying the same trick on her instead of on the lotus-leaves. She too looked like this lotus-leaf, beautiful, but unresponsive. The dew-drops had made her look extremely young and ephemeral. But there was no trace of joy or sorrow on her face. Nachiketa had tried to listen to her silence. She seemed to understand and smiled, a little sadly, as if to say....But no, he did not understand what she seemed to say. With a sudden surge of emotion he had put his arms around her and kissed her and then feeling assured that he had done the right thing with this gesture, he had run away to his world of sounds and silences, turning for a moment to look at her with an implicit promise of coming back.

But today as he hurried toward their cottage he thought more of his father than of her; but not in the way he thought of her, however. He never had to think of her, just as he never had to think of himself, or of the river, or of the sky, the nights and the mornings. They were simply there. They made no demands and were unending like his mother, and yet were there within the grasp of his embrace.

For the past one month his father had been busy calculating something with the almanacs spread before him. He was also busy taking measurements in the courtyard for a place to build the ritual fire. Nachiketa had been running around doing errands for him. Men who looked like solid mountains had come to help him prepare for the ceremony.

Nachiketa had once sat by his father watching them discuss something which he did not understand. He tried to copy their gestures as faithfully as he could and got so engrossed in the game that he failed to understand why one of them felt offended when he caught Nachiketa in his act of mimicry and why his father had turned to him in anger upon that.

Nachiketa knew that his father wanted many things. He saw him toiling day and night. At times he wanted some miracle to happen so that his father would forget the heavy books and the learned discussions and join him in his lonely excursions in the woods. Nachiketa's heart would go out to meet and seek his father out. But there was no place for him to occupy in his father's domain. He felt like an alien who had strayed into a territory the laws of which could not be fathomed and which yet asked him to comply. And very often Nachiketa violated those laws without being able to understand the severity of the punishment. He felt like a criminal who silently suffered, and suffered all the more intensely because he did not understand what his crime was.

Forests and streams and the changing skies became his companions. They spoke to him in their silence. They healed his wounds and gave him a strange strength: a strength that came from an all-abiding love. At night, upon waking up in the middle of it, he would stare in amazement at his father's countenance. Those lines of deep trouble and frustrations would take on the shape of an undecipherable sorrow. At such moments Nachiketa would almost see the likeness of the tempestuous trees in the forest when they were stilled into silence. He would remember the ceaseless toil of that sleeping heart during the day. Nachiketa's pure heart and tender soul would stoop in compassion over that agonized, anguished human who was his father. The two souls would be suspended in a closeness, one awake, the other asleep. In one there were no desires, and the other lacerated by unfulfilled dreams. Nachiketa would stare long at the dimly lit features through the intervening shadows cast by the trees outside the cottage-window.

In the morning the room would be bright and noisy. The vision of the night would be replaced by the sight of his father moving about the house in immaculately clean white clothes. His strident voice would belie all that he spoke to Nachiketa in the space of the night.

Today as Nachiketa sat on the bank of the river all those thoughts rushed through his mind like a vision of fleeting shapes of clouds. On his way he felt lonely and neglected. A while ago when he had left the cottage to reach the river-bank he was prancing like a young colt. Now he was walking with a ponderous gait, gazing at each pebble on the ground and sometimes kicking at the bigger ones vigorously.

When he reached the cottage he found his mother fatigued and busy. As usual she was making mistakes after mistakes and in rectifying them, was making blunders. His father was now seated near the sacrificial altar and repeating the words of the priest of the ceremony, while at the same time giving oblations and offerings of black sesame seeds and ghee to the altar of fire. Nachiketa tip-toed and sidled up to him, and then very unobtrusively sat by him in subdued silence. The sound of the mantras was rising and falling with a steady rhythm. It filled the atmosphere with a vibrating energy. Nachiketa sat in rapt attention, watching his father's actions, gestures and expressions. He had heard from the discussions he had listened to that this sacrifice was called 'Kamya vishvajit'- one which would reward the sacrificer with the world of his desire. Only, he still could not make out the nature of the world that his father desired. He wanted to ask, but knew what his father was going to say: "Stop asking questions!"

Poor and emaciated brahmins sat in a row on the right side. Each one was given something as a gift. Nachiketa watched in silent wonder. He would try to guess what the next gift would be. His mother had told him that almost everything that belonged to his father would be gifted away and that his father would be blessed and get the desired reward. Only, she did not know what reward he desired. Nachiketa was shocked out of his reverie when he heard a heart-rending cry from the cow-stead. It was his favourite cow Kapila, and sure enough, it was she being dragged to the courtyard where the ceremony was being held. Two hefty brahmins were pulling her towards the courtyard. The cow was resisting and kicking with all the fury she could muster. But soon her resistance gave way and she sank to the ground, foaming at the mouth with exhaustion and fatigue. Nachiketa got up in a split moment and rushed to her side. She had been old and sick for the last many days and he had been tending her. Surely, his father wasn't going to push her out in this state! He stroked her forehead and though she was almost in a daze, she recognized his touch and responded weakly. Then she opened her eyes, as if to bid him farewell. Her silent look pierced his heart. True, he had understood silence. But the silence he had heard till then was benign, full of some unknown benediction and promise. This silence was totally unknown to him. This too was the silence of benediction, but so different! It simply said, "This is my lot, my little benefactor, and so be it! I must accept it. With all the gratitude I bless thee. Now let me go."

In a flash, Nachiketa understood all this. There was the sound of something cracking at the back of his mind and then a deluge. One after another, all their emaciated cows, the whole herd of them, was led out of the stable. Their heart-rending cries drowned the steady chant of the mantras and seemed to make a mockery of it.

Nachiketa came back to his seat and sat there in stunned silence. He could hear nothing, not even silence. Within him there was chaos and din of voices. He had lost something else with the loss of that cow. He had lost his world of harmony. Nothing belonged to him then; not even his own inner world. His father would trample upon it at his will. His dreams of communion with his father were false. He had never been allowed to step into his father's dominion, but one day he had hoped to take his father into the world that he had discovered-the world of the silent rivers, the skies, the forests, the night-sky.

But his father had shown him how vain he had been in cherishing this dream, because that was not the world that his father desired. Nachiketa could now see clearly what his father desired. He desired power, not strength. In one stroke he had demonstrated to him what power could do in a moment.

Today as Nachiketa sat on the bank of the river all those thoughts rushed through his mind like a vision of fleeting shapes of clouds. On his way he felt lonely and neglected. A while ago when he had left the cottage to reach the river-bank he was prancing like a young colt. Now he was walking with a ponderous gait, gazing at each pebble on the ground and sometimes kicking at the bigger ones vigorously.

When he reached the cottage he found his mother fatigued and busy. As usual she was making mistakes after mistakes and in rectifying them, was making blunders. His father was now seated near the sacrificial altar and repeating the words of the priest of the ceremony, while at the same time giving oblations and offerings of black sesame seeds and ghee to the altar of fire. Nachiketa tip-toed and sidled up to him, and then very unobtrusively sat by him in subdued silence. The sound of the mantras was rising and falling with a steady rhythm. It filled the atmosphere with a vibrating energy. Nachiketa sat in rapt attention, watching his father's actions, gestures and expressions. He had heard from the discussions he had listened to that this sacrifice was called 'Kamya vishvajit'- one which would reward the sacrificer with the world of his desire. Only, he still could not make out the nature of the world that his father desired. He wanted to ask, but knew what his father was going to say: "Stop asking questions!"

Poor and emaciated brahmins sat in a row on the right side. Each one was given something as a gift. Nachiketa watched in silent wonder. He would try to guess what the next gift would be. His mother had told him that almost everything that belonged to his father would be gifted away and that his father would be blessed and get the desired reward. Only, she did not know what reward he desired. Nachiketa was shocked out of his reverie when he heard a heart-rending cry from the cow-stead. It was his favourite cow Kapila, and sure enough, it was she being dragged to the courtyard where the ceremony was being held. Two hefty brahmins were pulling her towards the courtyard. The cow was resisting and kicking with all the fury she could muster. But soon her resistance gave way and she sank to the ground, foaming at the mouth with exhaustion and fatigue. Nachiketa got up in a split moment and rushed to her side. She had been old and sick for the last many days and he had been tending her. Surely, his father wasn't going to push her out in this state! He stroked her forehead and though she was almost in a daze, she recognized his touch and responded weakly. Then she opened her eyes, as if to bid him farewell. Her silent look pierced his heart. True, he had understood silence. But the silence he had heard till then was benign, full of some unknown benediction and promise. This silence was totally unknown to him. This too was the silence of benediction, but so different! It simply said, "This is my lot, my little benefactor, and so be it! I must accept it. With all the gratitude I bless thee. Now let me go."

In a flash, Nachiketa understood all this. There was the sound of something cracking at the back of his mind and then a deluge. One after another, all their emaciated cows, the whole herd of them, was led out of the stable. Their heart-rending cries drowned the steady chant of the mantras and seemed to make a mockery of it.

Nachiketa came back to his seat and sat there in stunned silence. He could hear nothing, not even silence. Within him there was chaos and din of voices. He had lost something else with the loss of that cow. He had lost his world of harmony. Nothing belonged to him then; not even his own inner world. His father would trample upon it at his will. His dreams of communion with his father were false. He had never been allowed to step into his father's dominion, but one day he had hoped to take his father into the world that he had discovered-the world of the silent rivers, the skies, the forests, the night-sky.

But his father had shown him how vain he had been in cherishing this dream, because that was not the world that his father desired. Nachiketa could now see clearly what his father desired. He desired power, not strength. In one stroke he had demonstrated to him what power could do in a moment.

Power could demolish in a moment what strength had created over those few years of understanding with love and succour. Nachiketa sobbed silently as he looked at this man who was his father, this man who was performing the ritual, supremely unconcerned about what he was sacrificing so long as he believed that it was going to give him something in return. After all, he was giving away what belonged to him.

Nachiketa looked meaninglessly into the blazing, dancing flames of the altar-fire. All his dreams, his inner sanctuary, everything in it was set ablaze. Nothing belonged to him. All his childlike desires were reduced to ashes. What was he then? Did he belong to himself? Or did he belong to his father?

He tugged at his father's shawl and said, "Father, do I belong to you?"

"Yes", there came the authoritarian answer, and then the usual reprimand: "Stop questioning!"

Nachiketa wondered at this mighty power which took away from him even the right to question. How was he to understand the meaning of this if even his questions did not belong to him? How was he to know unless he asked? Now everything depended on the answer to this question at that moment. Did he belong to himself? If he belonged to himself he would know the meaning of this all. He would know the meaning of silence. But if he belonged to his father what was he? Like a mirror, Nachiketa's pure consciousness reflected a strange likeness between himself and the cow. And suddenly an inexorable logic took possession of his mind. The cow seemed to know her lot in life. She had accepted it meekly. Will he be able to accept it? No. He must know who was going to claim him. He tugged at his father's shawl again and asked him the question that held in balance all that mattered to him.

"Father, who are you going to give me to?"

"Nachiketa, stop questioning."

"No, Father, please tell me. I must know."

At this his father brushed him aside and said, "Go away from here. Don't be a nuisance, or I will give you away to Yama."

"But oh, why Father? Am I of no use to you?"

His father, who was too busy to understand the loaded meaning of the question, turned his attention to the instructions being given to him by the priest of the ceremony at that moment. He threw a glance at Nachiketa in exasperation and said heedlessly, "Oh, I have no use for you and your questions. Yes, I have given you away to Yama. Now that's the answer. Go away from here."

(A page which formed a vital link in the script is missing here, appropriately perhaps. This rupture in the narrative was a coincidence and like certain coincidences it created a vacuum within which one can write everything or nothing. It also made me think over my father's aversion to my story-telling skills. He did not want that I should understand pain and sorrow. My Guru was perhaps happy that at last I was fit to be a disciple.

In the postmodern techniques of scripting, a rupture in the narrative is also a point of loose ends which let the reader in and write the script. Whatever it may be, a coincidence seized as a moment for introspection, a rupture, or a technique, the narrative has to go on.)

Nachiketa read a sign in the words uttered by his father. His childish mind was not equipped to understand the nuances of the adult language. His world had taken a trauma. Fables and parables are not allegories to a child who has just begun to understand the world and its language. His reality was broken. He had no language to communicate the massive impact of it. He wanted now to meet Yama, the divinity of Death, face to face. If it was Yama who was going to claim him, he belonged to Yama. He felt drawn in love to Yama.

The night was long and restless for Nachiketa. He stayed wide awake and stared into the heart of that night, defenceless and bewildered. He closed his eyes. It made no difference, within and without, all was the same. Is this what they call death? Is this what he loved?

Suddenly he realized that it was not his own death that he feared. How could he die? He breathed his own name slowly. Each breath filled him with a strength that was beyond hope and time. He realized that at that moment something had happened to him out of time.

Yes, he was free to choose and he had the strength to choose. And now it did not matter where he lived. In that single night he had come a long way to belong to Death, because he did not belong anywhere. Now he belonged to himself. It was all the same now, here or there, or anywhere; in the woods or in the world of sacrificial rites and strife; Nachiketa would be Nachiketa.

Nachiketa was conquered by Nachiketa. Nachiketa was beautiful; Nachiketa was strong, inexhaustible. No longer would he be banished; no longer would he shy away from the world. His mother, his cow, his father, everything came back to him and he gave them love, infinite love. But not by living here. He must break away from it all.

....

It was a long, long journey, alone to an unknown destination, a journey in search of the meaning of life, and strangely in search of Death. The boy went on and on in search of Death so that great Master would reveal to him the meaning of life. He had left behind the silent rivers, the changing skies, the humming forests to understand the silence beyond it all.

Driven by a lunatic force, he went ahead as if borne on the crest of a deafening tide, inebriate with the desire to know. He was being washed away to the feet of the inevitable. Mornings brought sunrise and with the sun going down he would feel the sea-gulls sweeping across the sky, singing a desperate song to ease the tedium of lonely flights to unknown lands. The boy would gaze at the horizon till the ever-widening blue conquered his vision and sleep too became a sightless plunge into the Blue. His lust or the horizon made him forget that the land never ends and the sky never begins.

Thus Nachiketa travelled for three days and three nights and then dropped down in sheer exhaustion and fatigue.

Myriad forms fleeted past his vision in that moment, his mother's silent face, the river-bed, the lotus-leaf, the silent, suffering in the eyes of Kapila, and then his father's volcanic eruption: "Go, I have given thee to Yama, The god of Death." The next moment Nachiketa could no longer hear silence; he became part of it.

No one knew the old man. He avoided being seen and lived in his cottage at the far end of the thick forest. No one knew who he was and whence he came. A few who had happened to stray into that part of the forest saw him, but none could talk to him. His silence seemed unfathomable. But those few who saw him were hardly the same when they came back to their village to their human abode.

Sometimes unknown and unseen, he would come out of his dark cottage on a bright afternoon and sit basking in the courtyard, looking into the distance, as if waiting for some lone way-farer to come, and lift the age-long spell and bring to life the shrunken silence to dance on his wild flute-notes.

Those who had seen him told others afterwards that one might see him suddenly face to face and catch him smiling. But that smile would not be like anything you had seen before. It was a benign smile that accepted you and set you free, and thereafter one could not belong to anything in this world and yet be a part of it.

For three days and three nights the old man had been away from the cottage. When he came back he saw a human form lying in a heap at the door of the cottage. On going nearer, he found it to be a boy of about seven years, probably of the brahmin lineage. It was obvious that the boy had barely made it to the gate of the cottage and then collapsed from hunger and exhaustion. The old man looked long and steadily into that tender countenance, now immobile, but still retaining its fluid transparency. He bent over the child with silent compassion and stroked the matted hair and the little forehead that had gathered layers of dust. Then lifting him gently, he carried him inside. The old man sat motionless until he saw a slight manifestation of life in that limp body and then watched with interest the gradual awakening of the senses until all the senses reaffirmed the existence of body and the world around them.

The boy opened his eyes and saw a pair of eyes watching him serenely in utter silence. No, this wasn't his father.

"Are you the one I am looking for?"

"Who are you looking for my dear?" The old man asked gently without a trace of astonishment.

"Why, you must be Yama. I had set out in search of you!"

"Indeed? Do I look like Yama to you? I don't know what I look like!"

Nachiketa silently wondered. True, he did not know either what Yama looked like! He stared at this serene face and could think no more. All that he could understand at that moment was that he wanted to be claimed and at that moment it did not matter who was to claim him! Slowly, a tiny hand lifted itself. So slight was its movement that it was scarcely visible to the eye. But an old, wrinkled hand, strong and steady, grasped it and Nachiketa lay trustful in the old man's lap, assured and asleep.

Nachiketa spent the formative years of his life with this man who seemed to exist in a land beyond life and death. By now Nachiketa knew every brook, waterfall, and tree in that hilly region. After the last batch of monsoon clouds had departed, the winter would set in. Then the old man would wake Nachiketa before sunrise and the two would explore the hills for herbs. Their search would sometimes take them to the crest of the hill. Sometimes they would rest under a tree and watch the crowns of the neighbouring hills until the first rays of the morning brought to light their rough surfaces and threw into relief the multiple shades of colours that had so far been merged in one purple sheet of darkness. Below, one would never be able to fathom the depth of the valley.

Once Nachiketa got up from deep sleep, thinking it was dawn. He found the old man sitting cross-legged, silently facing the east. A delicate tinge of pink in the purple sky had deluded Nachiketa. He sat near the old man and stared into the dark. The old man gently stroked his head and said, "This is a false dawn. But do not fall asleep again. Stay awake and you will see how it will change into a real dawn. It is a beautiful experience." So Nachiketa sat there, watching the sky. Sleep overwhelmed him. It was a painfully long interval before the first rays of the sun started to ascend the sky. In the interval he felt drowsy and longed to go back to sleep, thinking that the darkness would never end. But then came the moment when the hint of the lustrous orb of the sun appeared behind the hill and soon the entire sphere began to throb and expand with growing light.

The old man smiled at him and said, "My friend, you will always remember what you have learnt in this moment here and now, and it will fill your life with light as it did today".

These days the old man was mostly confined to the four walls of their cottage. Nachiketa, now young and strong, had been busy collecting life-giving herbs for him. His search would take him to far off hills and valleys, to places which he had never known to exist before. It was an unusual experience for Nachiketa to wander alone thus. When alone, he would sometimes think of the past he had left behind, his father, mother, the fateful day on which he broke away from all of that life, his journey to the unknown...He would be arrested in his meandering thoughts by the reminder of the gentle, soothing words of the old man. In the moments when grief had seemed to overwhelm him, when the effort to connect himself with his origin had proved futile, the old man would say, "Do not try to remember the past, nor think of what is to come. Think of here and now, my boy. Do not chase shadows. Time is ever present. "

Nachiketa would then stare at the herbs he had collected. He would refrain from asking the unasked question:"What was he going to do with these herbs? He could not yet distinguish very well the remedial ones from the harmful. He had to place them before the old man who would feel them with his trembling fingers, smell them and explain the properties of each of them. His eye-sight had weakened and Nachiketa knew that he could scarcely distinguish between objects except by their feel. Looking at him, Nachiketa began to fear the knowledge that seemed to dwell in the deep recesses of the old man's heart which Nachiketa, as yet, had not begun to fathom.

Nachiketa was now most often left to his own devices to fathom the answers to the questions that arose in his hours of deep meditation. He often wondered if the old man knew the direction of his thoughts and his quest, and still held back the answers for reasons of his own. Nachiketa was almost a child when he was brought by providence to the door of the old man, really to die, but perhaps the providence, or perhaps the old man, did not let him die. His childish faith had led him here not really in search of what the world calls 'death', but in search of answers which the child in him had believed to be in the trust of the divinity called 'Yama'. At that time the old man came and gave him life, not death. He wanted to be claimed by death; he was claimed by life. All these years he was cut off from the life of society. He and the old man were the creatures of the forest. The forest knew them and they knew the forest. The forest knew what they needed and gave them in plenty. It was so plentiful that they had forgotten what it is like to be in lack of something.

The old man did not teach him anything, but Nachiketa learnt everything by way of osmosis. He absorbed the old man's agility of the body and the mind. He absorbed his way of synchronizing decision and action. He absorbed the old man's virtual invisibility as he reflected on a phenomenon. He understood the marvellous ways in which he disguised his reality when he had to appear differently to the world out there. He had soon realized that the old man was an ace marksman and a good hunter who never missed his target. Living with him, Nachiketa had no memories of his roots. They lingered in his mind as pictures recalled from a dream. He had lived the years of his childhood in that state of virtual amnesia. But as self-awareness increased, he started thinking about what he had left behind. He remembered that he had dreams of an idyllic world of ideas which he had longed to share with his father and his father's discordant relationship with the world did not let him in. In his hours of meditation he was often confused as to the nature of his thoughts about his father. As he grew up he developed the practice of concentration and contemplation. But the process of growing up was tied up with a growing realization of his father's heart and the mind. He was confused about those thoughts because he did not know whether they were distractive and needed to be banished from the focus of meditation or whether they needed to be tamed and understood fully. Often, he felt his father's hand touch his heart, as if that touch was trying to say something that transcended words. The memory of his father's strident and commanding, almost terrifying voice would wake up and gradually shade off into an ardent whisper. That whisper seemed to have a voice that desperately called for attention. Nachiketa did not know what to do at such moments. He had no experience of dealing with such feelings. He had no way of establishing a contact with a person who had once ruled over his life and was now relegated to the domain of imagination. He had no way of determining if his perception of that whisper was real or a fragment of imagination.

The old man was neither curious nor perturbed over Nachiketa's past. As Nachiketa grew up and understood his environment, its perspective and meaning began to grow upon his consciousness. He did not know whether the old man's apparent apathy was empathy raised to an all-encompassing universal consciousness. Nachiketa as yet had no ability to merge with that dimension where, at this stage of his growth, he felt, God alone could dwell.

It was the dark fortnight of the month of Chaitra, the beginning of summer when Nachiketa sat alongside the old man in meditation. His mind was not at peace, thinking of the past and the deteriorating health of the old man who had seen him through all along his lonely path of life. Nachiketa had begun to feel the need to reconcile with, or at least to understand, his past which he had left behind in search of 'the ultimate ', the 'Yama', who he believed was going to claim him. He sat beside the old man who was in deep meditation in that dark hour of the night, serene and lost to the world. The serenity of the night-sky had absorbed the old man's spirit so completely that he seemed to melt and flow into it.

Nachiketa closed his eyes again and let his mind and spirit be carried away into the infinity of the night, and the old man's presence in it ceased to be felt. Nachiketa became one with the breath of the old man and that of the night. Everything breathed as one single entity. Nachiketa extricated himself out of that totality with an effort of the will. In that moment he wondered whether the old man was in fact an astral being, an alien who did not belong to the world that moved, lived and dissolved in small fragments, not at once, but in isolated phases and moments, with each individual being. Indeed, this was the way 'Yama', the astral god of Death, controls the universe, thought Nachiketa. He marvelled at the unflawed wisdom which had led him in search of Yama, in the belief that Yama was the ultimate Master who held answers to all that appeared mysterious to the child Nachiketa in the incomplete understanding of life that the human beings displayed in their behaviour, deeds and actions, in their greed and grasping, in their fears and anxieties. For the child that he was then, his father was the epitome of all humanity. In the silence of the night Nachiketa saw with a greater clarity than before, the path that had brought him here to the old man. It was a light that he had shared with his father, as if since a time without beginning. The child Nachiketa had not known the use of reason, but still, his intuitive light refused to be obscured by his father's world which was ordered by the tyranny of ignorance. Standing behind both, his father and him, was the unseen presence of Death, watching over their journey silently. Nachiketa wondered why it was that his father chose the way of ambition and why he chose the path towards Death. Suddenly he saw the old man in a new light. From the very moment he was obscured as he lay unconscious at the door of this cottage, his inner teacher had taken over completely, resuscitated his spirit, and tirelessly brought him back to the radiance and the spaciousness of his being, without for a moment letting go of his hand. That inner teacher who had dwelt inside him all along had manifested itself to him as the outer form of the old man. That encounter, which he almost believed to be with Death, was the momentous miracle of his life.

Nachiketa had returned to the cottage after a busy day at the village-market after selling the medicinal herbs. He was busy counting the day's earning when he became aware of the old man sitting next to him and looking at him contentedly.

Nachiketa looked at him fixedly for a moment. The old man said, "This was the day of the year when twenty years back providence had dropped you here at my doorstep to die."

"But you did not let me die, "said Nachiketa.

The old man laughed. He watched the rugged, buoyant look on the young man's face and said, "Your Guru would not let you die before you live out the span."

Nachiketa did not look up from his counting but he paused for a brief moment. The old man seemed restrained. There was silence for awhile. Nachiketa was about to get up when the old man said, "I am glad to see that you have mastered all the secrets of my trade now. "

Nachiketa stared into the old man's eyes and laughed.

"Not all, old man; I have yet to extract a lot more."

The old man smiled mysteriously and said with a little laugh, "Do you believe that I have a treasure still hidden somewhere around here?"

Nachiketa's mind floated over that little laugh and the restraint behind it. He said, "I know, and I still cannot forget. Providence apart, I had come here in search of something which I believed was held in the hands of Death alone. You were that to me: Yama, the highest Guru of mankind, hiding behind it all, holding all answers. But mankind would not have them from you."

"The mankind would never have them because I would not dispense with them, not before I make them receive the initiation through fire which is life", said the old man.

Nachiketa said, "But I want to go through fire with all the answers known to me. Those will be my shield. Why do you withhold them from me? Am I not dear enough to you?"

The old man was silent. He looked at him as if his silence was the answer.

He said, "Go back to the life you have left unlived. You will discover all answers."

Nachiketa understood. The Highest Guru was there before him and yet he was being put to the hardest test of life.

There was a stone wall which he could not break. It was a moment which demanded the essence of his being.

The old man said, "Do not ask questions. Ask for boons and I have plenty to give. Ask for what matters to all living beings—the best of the life on this earth, wealth, longevity, love. I will give all that to you"

Nachiketa said, "And still I will not know what to do with all that. You know I am ill-equipped to put it to use."

"You will learn. It's not hard to find out how," said the old man.

Nachiketa thought of his father and all those who surrounded his father at various levels of existence. He wondered if his father had found by now what he was seeking. He realized what his father sought and did not find. He was astonished at the simplicity of the answer. It was love he did not find. Nachiketa experienced all that anguish all over again.

The old man read all that was passing through Nachiketa's mind as he thought of the boon of life.

Nachiketa turned to the old man who seemed to hold all the mysterious possibilities within his power at that moment.

"I have nothing to ask for myself, but I want my father to be happy," said Nachiketa.

"And if you think that wealth and longevity was what would make him happy ask for it and you will have them for your father," said the old man.

Nachiketa looked at the old man and saw compassion in his eyes but still not all that there was which he could give but would not unless asked for.

He said after a while, "Yes, I ask for wealth and longevity for him because that was what he was seeking and told me, that must be sought after by the wise." After a pause he said, "But I want him to have peace. That is the reason I want his wish to be fulfilled."

This time the old man was quick to answer. He said, "Will he have peace with all the wealth and the power that comes with wealth? No my son. He still needs you. Go back and find out why he needs you"

Nachiketa pondered over this oracular command. He had sought his roots. He did not find them in the soil where he was born. He had accomplished a long flight and reached here. He had been nurtured and brought up by this man whom he had believed to be Yama. He had learnt life under the shadow of 'Death'. Where were his roots now?

He spoke, without looking at the old man, "You are asking a bird to leave the sky and go back to the cage."

The old man said, "No, not to the cage. You will go back to complete what you were sent here to do"

Nachiketa said, "I have a choice, old man. You cannot take away my freedom now. "

The old man said, "Yes, you are still free and forever free. Your freedom is with you wherever you may be. This is precisely the time when you have to be reminded of it. You had used it once in the past to find yourself. That was your liberation. You had broken your shackles to find liberation in what you thought was your Death. You did not realize then that it was not an easy way out. But Yama, the Highest Guru knows. He knows what you have learnt and what you have yet to learn and also knows how much you can learn in one life-time. He only leaves you free to find your path."

Nachiketa said, "Then do not ask me to go back. I have found my path. It does not lead me back. I have been uprooted from that soil."

The old man said, "No, you are a different kind of a tree now. Your roots are in the open, infinite sky now and you will carry them wherever you will go. Your roots are in your soul, in your mind and your mind and soul are being nourished by that infinite consciousness which is your sky now. Don't you realize? You had touched the realm of Death and turned away from there by me, not without reason. "

Nachiketa looked at the old man. He was serene. For a while Nachiketa remained in that serenity in silence. The bond of love was overwhelming. He said, "You are Life in Death for me. Will you not come with me if I have to go from here?"

The old man said, "Now I am always with you, because your roots are with me, in the sky. "

There was a smile on the old man's face as he said this and there was a new-born beauty in it.

He said, "You did not care about your branches. Now with your roots in the sky and your branches spreading in this sphere, you are a new man, strong, nourished with the new knowledge of freedom. Your branches will not die hereafter."

There was a prolonged meditative gap in their dialogue. Nachiketa gathered his powers of determination to fight off a command coming from the person whom he had chosen to occupy the position of the highest guru of his life.

He said with a drastic defiance,' I shall not go back to a world that has no place for me. That world had rejected me long back when they did not even know what rejection meant to the child that I was. I have neither the energy nor the will to go to that world and beg them to take me into their folds."

The old man responded with the knowledge that this moment was the moment of the greatest truth for the boy. He said, "The world cannot reject you my son. Now is the beginning of your journey. The days you spent here was the time of recuperation. You have not realized your strength yet, and you will not realize it until you test it against the hostile world. You touched the realm of Death once, not to fall into a dull, protective shell of inertia, a sense of false stability. Face the new path with the vibrancy that I am giving you now. It is my gift, Yama's gift which no other blessing can surpass. You have the unique destiny of returning to the world of the living, with a life reinforced at the hands of Death. You will walk the earth with a life superimposed. Children blessed by me have no fear. They have lived under my shadow and released into the world to play their part. I do not let them come back to me before they play it. It is like walking on the razor's edge. But if you exercise your choice wisely, it will neither harm nor hurt. Be alert at the crossroads, and do not choose the path of least resistance. Knife out your existence, if necessary. Impart the lesson of fortitude to those around you. I shall be there to meet you at the journey's end."

The old man paused. They did not have the need to look at each other. In that silence Nachiketa saw the terrain of the life left behind and the one that was to come in a clear new light. A great serenity reigned at that moment between them which was a source of stability and strength for Nachiketa. His Master had spoken the final word. Hereafter the Master had no need to speak.

His Silence would surpass Speech.

....

The next morning Nachiketa got up and came out to look around. The eastern sky was all aglow. He went in. He must kindle the fire and heat water for the old man's bath. He will have to be helped to some food also.

Nachiketa stepped inside. The old man lay peaceful in his bed. The morning sun was shining warm upon his face. Every wrinkle upon it seemed to define and decode the mystery of his life to Nachiketa. For a moment Nachiketa gazed at him in awe and reverence and then bent down and touched his forehead. The old man seemed to acknowledge the touch and smile in benediction. Nachiketa's hand rested on the forehead for awhile and then Nachiketa understood. He gazed at the old man as though at infinity and then silently pulled the sheet over his face...

THE END.

The Myth of a River

There is a legend in India, not a very well-known one, woven around a river called Narmada: a river which has its origin at a place called Amar Kantaka in Central India. Most rivers in India have mysterious origins and as they flow down and enrich the soil on their banks, they merge with the lives of the people living around on their banks. Countless number of generations have watched them in awe and bowed down before the mystery of life which we call 'river'. They give a life and a meaning to rivers in the legends and myths which they weave around them.

Narmada is an implacable, angry river. But to see her in the full-moon night when people dedicate little lamp-lights to her waters is incredibly beautiful. Endless treacle of small lights gives itself up in a surrender to the silent river and flows with the current. The lights of the little lamps as they flow into the expanse of the waters flicker, tremble, as they are carried away by the river. The moon does not seem to take gently or kindly to them. The moon-beams seem to come down heavily on them. The lamp-lights get dimmer as they move up, unable to compete with the luminous moon-beams, they flicker and disappear on the expanse of the river. Far away, where the river bends, the moonlight is enchanting. It is remote and silent. Here, right in front of you, the expanse of the river is beautiful; the moonlight is beautiful, and everything is beautiful in itself. But there, where the river bends, life seems mysterious. The moon alone reigns there.

The legend of Narmada has lived in the minds of the peasants with an archetypal reality. It goes like this: Narmada: the present river was, once upon a time, a princess, the only child of a king called Amar Kantaka who is now recognized as the place where the river Narmada originates. Her father had wanted to give her in marriage to a powerful prince ruling on the other side of his kingdom who was known as Shona. Today, Shona is the name of the male river which flows down from the opposite side of Narmada. In India the rivers which resemble the sea in their expanse are called male rivers. Shona is one such male river. Unfortunately, Amar Kantaka did not live to see his daughter get married to the prince of his choice. He died a little before the day on which the marriage was scheduled to take place. The mantle of kingdom fell on the shoulders of the young princess. She took up the rein as the new queen and thereafter she had no time to look up from her duties and responsibilities. She was just and fair to all and kind-hearted as a mother to all her people. But the responsibilities were weighing her down.

Shona did not have a chance to see her during her ordeal. After some time, thinking that she might have come out of her grief, he sent her a ring to show her that he had not forgotten his promise. Narmada wore it with gratitude on her finger. She sent her messenger to him and got a date fixed for their marriage.

Narmada was eager to see the man of her dreams as the day of the marriage approached near. The place where Shona had arrived and camped was not very far from where she was. But the custom and the protocol explicitly forbade her to see him before the day of the marriage. She mustered courage and decided to send him a ring that was her personal belonging. It was going to be her token of love for him. She yearned to know what he looked like, how he conducted himself and so on. In her eagerness and impatience she took an impulsive decision to send her personal attendant Zola, who was also her bosom friend, on this mission to Shona, with a priceless ring from the vault of her treasure.

Zola belonged to one of the Indian village communities who were well-known for their ability to dig out people's intimate secrets in the course of inconsequential chatter. Zola was well-versed in this art. Having lived close to the princess, she had acquired refinement. But her greatest asset was her beauty.

When Zola reached Shona's camp she found him standing outside the royal tent. Zola was enamoured to see him. Love got the better of her. Now she was just a woman, not the trusted messenger of the queen. The ring which was the token of the queen's love was already sitting on her finger audaciously. The young man saw her; she blushed and began to rearrange the folds of her sari on her shoulder coyly. As she was engaged in the act, the ring on her finger caught the sunlight and reflected it back. The luminous diamond in the ring could belong to none but a queen. When Shona saw it he was certain that the woman who wore it was the princess he was betrothed to. He was overjoyed, and mistaking her to be his bride, took Zola in. Everything happened just the way Zola wished.

For many days they celebrated love and nothing but love. Time went by. One day the truth came to light. But by then Zola had conquered the prince. He was deep in love with the woman who was Zola. Zola was the reality, Narmada was a myth. He was aware of his commitment but he lived for the moment now.

Days passed. Zola did not return. The story that the secret messenger brought back to Narmada was beyond belief. Narmada flew into a rage. She hated Shona. Joy was banished out of her life. She was now like a river out of bounds. She reached Shona's camp with a resolve to swallow him in the deluge. Her anger mounted as the things became plain to her. With one kick she settled the score with Zola and with another, she knocked down the powerful man that Shona was. Shona apologized and even promised to get rid of Zola, but Narmada refused to relent.

She declared her resolve to Shona, "Narmada will not marry a depraved man. All men are alike. Now you will see my resolve. I shall remain virgin for life. Get lost and get this wretched woman out of my sight. "

Shona walked away taking Zola with him. Narmada who was destined to flow east where her husband's home was, now turned her back on him and became westward bound. To this day she did not look back towards the east.

Now, looking after her subjects was the sole mission of her life. But the heart of Narmada is tied up in knots at various places in the course of her path. People say that even today when she comes across traitors, Narmada seethes with anger. There are deep, silent vortices in her backwaters which are undetected until you are close to them. They are swirling with rage and can suck unsuspecting humans into their depths. She flows with tremendous force between the precipitous rocks which flank both sides of her gushing stream. There is a rare spot where you chance to see Narmada resting quietly, exhausted and defeated. This is a place called Bhedaghat. It is a steep, precipitous, rocky region where she hurls herself down in a desperate fall. The steep rush into which the tremendous river hurls herself down on the rocks below, creates a mist. It is like a giant fountain of myriad shades of mist. And then, you watch her flowing further down after that stupendous leap, further and further over the level terrain until she reaches a zone of silence. Here her waters are silent and clear. You see her making her way, flowing on quietly between tall marble rocks guarding her on both sides. The pure white marble rocks guard the privacy of the woman who has found her solitude and after a phase of self-consuming sorrow, sleeps like an orphaned princess inside the majestic four walls of her palace. This is the most mysteriously beautiful spot in Narmada's volatile path of fury. This is the spot where her pride broke, her tears coursed down silently and she went beyond grief and joy. This is the place called Bhedaghat where terror and rage are silenced and a strange beauty is born.

The End.